Wonderwitch
goes to the dogs

Helen Muir

Illustrated by Linda Birch

MACDONALD YOUNG BOOKS

FOR PAT – *who is a bit of a witch herself*

Text copyright © Helen Muir 1995
Illustrations copyright © Linda Birch 1995

First published in 1995

First published in Great Britain in 1995
by Macdonald Young Books
Campus 400
Maylands Avenue
Hemel Hempstead
Herts HP2 7EZ

Typeset in 16/24pt Plantin by Goodfellow & Egan Ltd, Cambridge
Printed and bound in Portugal by Ediçoes ASA

British Library Cataloguing in Publication Data available.

ISBN: 0 7500 1697 3
ISBN: 0 7500 1698 1 (pb)

Wonderwitch
Goes To The Dogs

Things started disappearing from
Wonderwitch's house. She couldn't
understand it.

Some chocolates went. A pizza was
missing from her shopping bag. Then she
put a roast chicken on the supper table,
went to fetch the carrots and that was
gone!

"I expect it's Witch Wotnot up to her old tricks," Wonderwitch said crossly to her black cat. "She's always been greedy and she's looking much fatter lately, probably on my food. I'm going to set a trap for her."

She put a lamb chop on the window sill and hid behind the curtain. The black cat watched from a tree.

Suddenly, the bushes rustled. A long nose poked out and big teeth gobbled up the meat.

"By Jove!" the witch cackled. "Wotnot's got a lot more ugly!"

She went on laughing to herself. "I'll catch the old boot in a net next time."

When it was dark she put more food out and hid again. After a time the nose appeared. With a shout of glee she threw her net over it. "Heh!"

There was a struggle. The witch screamed. The thief was strong and hairy and growled angrily. The witch got tangled in the net herself and rolled into a flowerbed.

"Strike me pink!" she gasped, "It's not Wotnot. It's a dog!"

She was most excited. "It's a greyhound," she told the black cat. "The poor thing's lost." And she mixed a tasty dinner of scraps and gravy.

She stroked the dog's head and made a fuss of him. "Greyhounds run like the wind. I love 'em. I'll call him Flash."

The black cat wasn't at all pleased when Flash moved in. He spent a lot of time glaring from the top of the kitchen cupboard because the dog kept thinking he was an electric hare and chasing him round the house.

"I've had a smashing idea,"
Wonderwitch said. "Let's have a Dog
Show!" And she put posters up everwhere.

Bring Your Dog
& Win a Prize!

Competition for:
Best Dog
Happiest Dog
Fastest Dog!

"If there's a race, my Rover will win it,"
Witch Wotnot boasted, out for a walk with
her long-legged lurcher.

"Want a bet?" said Wonderwitch.

"My dear girl, I'll bet anything you like," said Wotnot, who didn't know Wonderwitch had a greyhound.

Wonderwitch smiled slyly. "If your dog wins you get *my* house. If he loses, I get *your* house."

Witch Wotnot nodded gleefully. "Done!" And she started Rover's training by jogging all the way home.

The Dog Show was a great success.
People really enjoyed it. Witch Windbag
came with her spaniel and Witch Wonky
with a rottweiler. There were four beagles,
five labradors, ten terriers, six dobermans,
three alsatians, two setters, ninety-one
mongrels and a sheepdog. The prize for
Happiest Dog was won by a red setter.
Best Dog was the sheepdog.

When it was time for the Fastest Dog race, Wonderwitch led Flash out. Other owners groaned. Witch Wotnot went white with shock.

Wagging and sniffing, the dogs were lined up. The electric hare came whizzing out and they were OFF! Flash went like the wind and won easily.

"You ratbag!" Wotnot shouted as she handed over the keys to her house.

Wonderwitch laughed so much she walked into a tree. "I won't turn you out, sweetiepie. Why not rent your house from me? I'll only charge you five hundred quid a week."

During the next few weeks, Witch Wotnot secretly bought a champion racing greyhound called Silver Streak.

"Let's have another race?" she cooed to Wonderwitch. "If I win I get my house back, plus a year's supply of dog food. If you win, I'll buy you the yacht of your dreams to sail round the world."

Wonderwitch turned her guffaw into a cough. "Ha . . . hoff! May the best dog win!"

Wonderwitch knew Wotnot would cheat this time so before the race she visited a cranky crone called Witch Warthead for bad spells and good advice.

Then, disguised as a litter bin, she laid two trails of Warthead's Magic Dog Scent down the course. The outside trail went straight to the winning post. The inside trail went off into the hedge.

She guessed Witch Wotnot would nab the inside track and she did. But when Wonderwitch saw Silver Streak, she danced with rage. Another greyhound! The old crook!

"May the best dog win!" Wotnot screeched. And her racing champ bounded off like a rocket.

When the dogs sniffed the magic scent,
Flash went straight and Silver Streak
swerved off. Behind the hedge Witch
Warthead was waiting on her broomstick,
unseen by human eyes and smelling like a
beef casserole.

As she dipped and dived to delay Silver
Streak, he sprang after her. He bit the
broomstick and shook the witch off. She
bounced into a gorse bush.

So while Wotnot shouted and
Wonderwitch smiled, Flash won!

In the distance Witch Warthead escaped onto a bus and a kindly passer-by led Silver Streak back across the field. "I've lost a greyhound myself," he said. "I'll make sure this dog finds his owner."

Wonderwitch didn't notice the man because she was so excited. "My yacht, please, dearie!" she cackled to Wotnot while she kissed Flash on the nose. "That's my boy!"

18

"No, that's MY boy!" said a voice behind her and Flash gave a yelp of joy. He jumped right into his owner's arms.

"So you haven't won then!" Wotnot said. "He's not your dog."

"But I loved him," Wonderwitch was in tears as Flash went off to his real home.

"It's lucky I've got you to talk to," she told the black cat at bedtime.

There was a snore from her pillow. The cat was fast asleep for the first time in weeks.

The Portraits

When Wonderwitch called on Witch Wotnot she found her painting a lovely picture of all her pets. Rover, the lurcher, and the greyhound, Silver Streak, her cat and her parrot. "Jolly nice!" Wonderwitch said. And it set her off.

She went home and painted three pictures. *Black Cat Up A Tree, Black Cat Eating Prawns* and *Black Cat Sleeping.*

"Jolly good indeed!" she said to herself.
But by the time she'd hung her portraits
round the house, she was tired of that.

"I need someone to paint *me*," she said.
"After all, I am a wonderwitch." So she
talked to the other witches and they all
agreed to have a go.

But their pictures of her were so
dreadful, they upset Wonderwitch. Not
one of them made her look grand enough.

Witch Windbag painted her in a red dress and tiara.

"Two out of ten," said Wonderwitch, "I look like a warthog."

Witch Wonky painted her in the bath with only one eye.

"Hopeless," she snapped. "This is not art."

In Witch Wildblood's portrait, she was being stung on the nose by a wasp. She took a run at the canvas and kicked it to bits.

The witch was too cross to speak for three days. She lay in bed eating jelly babies until she had an idea.

"The way to find a true artist," she told the black cat, "is to hold a school competition. The children can paint me because they'll be more honest. The winning portrait will be presented to the Town Hall but I'm not having any meddling from grown-ups who don't know how to behave."

Wonderwitch put on her jewels and a silver gown and went off to Ludlow House School where she was met by the Head, Mr Dobson-Dent.

"What an honour for us!" he smiled. "Our young artists are waiting in the assembly hall. We've put a chair on the platform so that they can all see you at our sittings. I hope you'll be warm enough?"

"Oh, I'm not taking my clothes off," she said.

"Dear me . . . no," shuddered Mr Dobson-Dent.

Wonderwitch gave the children a
majestic smile. "I want you to paint me as I
am. The *real* me. Tell the truth in your
portrait and you may win the prize."

While the children set to work on their
paintings, a troublesome boy called
Freddie Firth had an idea.

"We won't get the prize if we don't tell
the truth," he whispered to his friend, Carl
King. "Let's spy on her. Then our
pictures will be really great."

So the boys went to
Wonderwitch's house
and peeped through
the letterbox.

The witch was eating cream cakes and
playing football with the black cat.
Suddenly she made a very rude noise and a
shower of ping-pong balls popped out of
her mouth.

Freddie and Carl laughed so loudly they
had to hide in the bushes. When the witch
came out to see what the noise was, they
froze with fright.

"She's wicked!" they told the other children. Then they all started spying on her too.

What the children saw surprised them! Clare and Francesca watched her breakfasting on pancakes and raspberry ice cream on their way to school.

Lucy, Jay, Lani, Marlon and Samantha
fell in the nettles when Wonderwitch
threw washing-up water out of the
window. Simeon Smith
said she went to
the supermarket
disguised as a nun.

"I think she really
likes jokes," he said.
And all of them
spied her doing
something
odd.

The children's paintings were ready for the day of the exhibition but nobody had been allowed to see them. The Mayor was to pick the winner and Wonderwitch had invited all the nobs she'd ever heard of.

"This is a great occasion," she told Witch Wotnot. "My portrait will hang in a hundred homes."

She wore her tiara for the Mayor's speech.

"We thank you, dear lady," he said, "for your interest in schools and art. We will be proud to hang the winner's portrait in the Town Hall."

With that, he and Wonderwitch and all the guests stepped to the first painting which was by Freddie Firth.

Their jaws dropped.

A silence fell.

Wonderwitch was sliding down the banisters in a bikini!

FREDDIE FIRTH

The Mayor's eyes popped. The witch went purple. Wotnot giggled . . . then everybody started. They all rocked.

In Carl King's picture Wonderwitch was tying a basketful of bricks to Witch Wonky's broomstick.

Simeon Smith had painted her putting a cowpat on Witch Windbag's doorstep.

Each picture was worse than the last.

Poor Wonderwitch said: "I have a phone call to make," and left.

She went to bed for a week with the black cat on her tummy for comfort. But she heard them laughing at the Town Hall in her dreams.

Wonderwitch
J.P.

"What I like . . . " Wonderwitch said to
the black cat, "is . . . *judging*. I'm a very
good judge of witches. I can't stand 'em."

The black cat closed his eyes.

She sucked a jelly baby. "That lump
Wotnot laughed at my portraits. She
should have a punishment."

She ate ten more jelly babies. "I'd like to
push her through a hedge backwards," she
scowled. "I'd like to make her eat beetroot
and boot polish stuffed with nails."

She made soup in a black cauldron and took it round to Wotnot.

"A little something, my dear," she cooed, "to help you out."

"I can't thank you enough, sweet one," replied Wotnot. She set the table. "How kind of you. We'll eat it together."

Wonderwitch went home in a temper. "It didn't work," she told the black cat. "That foxy old dame does so many bad deeds, she believes everyone else is up to no good.

"She's given me nothing but trouble. This world has become a terrible place. More judges are needed and I want to be one."

It is not easy to become a high court judge but almost any sensible person can be a magistrate. Quite soon the witch was Wonderwitch J.P. (Justice of the Peace).

She got herself a wig and even wore it to go shopping. She could hardly wait for her first day in court.

36

Judging was as exciting as she'd
expected.

"Court rise!" the Clerk shouted and
everybody stood up as Wonderwitch sailed
to the bench, nodding and smiling.

"Wigs are not worn in a magistrates'
court," the Clerk whispered.

"It's not a wig," replied the witch who
didn't wish to take it off.

Her first case went well. A motorist had parked his car on a double yellow line.

"I'm ever so sorry, Your Wonder-worship," the man said.

She beamed. "That's all right." And she let him off because she liked the look of him.

She hummed while she waited for the next case because she was enjoying herself.

"Charles Edward Dobson-Dent!" shouted the Clerk.

Wonderwitch frowned. "Ha!" She had not forgotten the rude pictures of her from Ludlow House School.

"You were speeding, Mr. Dobson-Dent! This is most serious."

"I was late for a meeting with the Mayor, Your Worship, about my pupils' art exhibition at the Town Hall."

"No excuse," the witch barked. "You will write out one thousand times *Dobson-Dent is a roadhog*." She nearly laughed out loud.

"Judging keeps me jolly busy," Wonderwitch told the black cat. "There's no end of crime."

She didn't call on her friends any more so one day Witch Wotnot set out to see her.

In too much of a hurry to look where she was going, she crashed her broomstick into Mrs Coots' washing line.

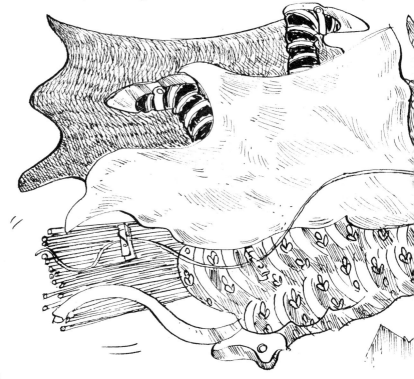

She grabbed at the wet clothes to save herself but she was going too fast. With blue knickers stuck on her head and black tights round her neck, she spun on through the kitchen window.

Smash . . . splinter . . . tinkle! The clothes line trailed in the mud.

Mrs Coots screamed. She called the police.

In court a police officer reported how
Wotnot had broken in to Mrs Coots' home
wearing stolen clothes.

"Shocking!" Wonderwitch said.
"Terribly shocking. And you laughed at the
Town Hall portraits too. Didn't
you . . . eh?" She pointed at Wotnot and
her voice squeaked as she tried hard not to
laugh herself. "The penalty for you
is . . . DEATH!"

Everybody gasped. Witch Wotnot made a tiny moan.

"I didn't mean to s..steal Mrs Coo..Coots' kn..kn..knickers. I was . . . was only ri..riding my broomstick."

"Come now, Mrs Wotnot," boomed Mr Bigbody, solicitor. "Are you trying to tell us that you are a witch?"

"Y..yes."

"A witch! Ha ha ha! But we don't believe in witches these days."

"WHAT?"
Wonderwitch leant
so far forward her
wig fell over her
eyes.

Mr Bigbody smiled scornfully. "If you're a witch, madam, why don't you turn me into a bar of soap?"

Wotnot said nothing.

"Well, if she won't," Wonderwitch suddenly shouted. "I WILL!"

There was a huge flash. Mr Bigbody
vanished. A bar of pink bath soap was on
his seat. A shocked murmur ran round the
court.

Wotnot visited Wonderwitch in the
police cells. "You'd better turn Mr
Bigbody back and get yourself out of
here."

Wonderwitch sighed. "Judging is *so* tiring. I can't remember the right spells."

So Witch Wotnot helped her with the words and they spoke them together.

Nippety nuppety noppety nap
Make Bigbody into a chap
Nippety nuppety noppety nee
Make us into something wee!

Two cockroaches scuttled out past the police officers and went home for a cup of tea.

Also by Helen Muir in the storybooks series:

Wonderwitch
Wonderwitch is tired of all her old spells, so she decides to try something quite different.

Wonderwitch and the Rooftop Cats
The crazy witch decides to set up in business, starting with the cat industry!

The Twenty-Ton Chocolate Mountain
Mr Mcweedie doesn't teach the children much about reading or adding up. Instead he tells them about spaghetti trees, singing sunflowers – and the Twenty Ton Chocolate Mountain.

Magic Mark
George wants to be a magician when he grows up. But when he tries out his spells they always end in disaster . . .

Ask for Storybooks at your local bookshop, or for more information write to: The Sales Department, Macdonald Young Books, Campus 400, Maylands Avenue, Hemel Hempstead HP2 7EZ.